W9-BMV-003

FGHIJK

QRSTU

ABCDE

LMNOP

Minnesota is filled with fantastic and beautiful things to see and do. Just follow the **A, B, C's,** there is an amazing adventure waiting for you!

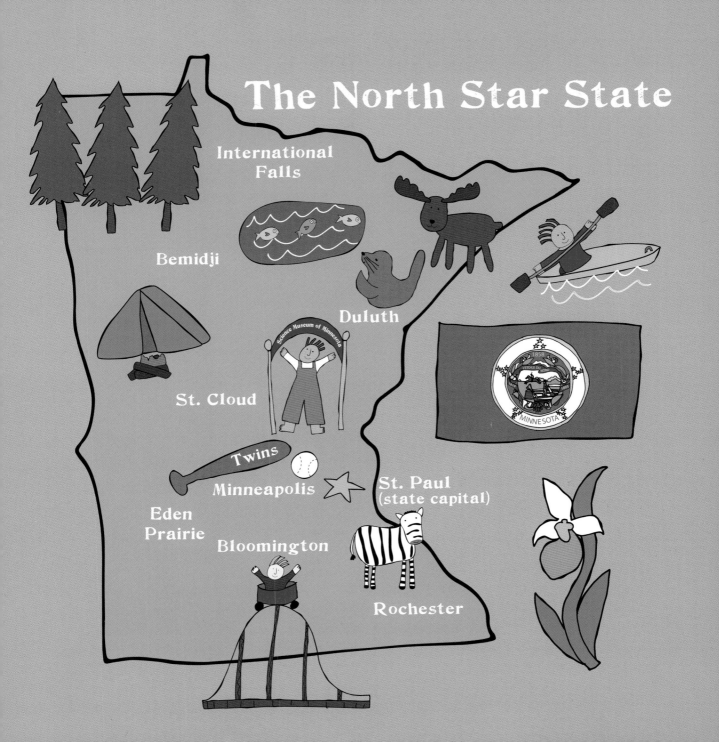

The North Star State

International Falls

Bemidji

Duluth

St. Cloud

Science Museum of Minnesota

Twins

Minneapolis

Eden Prairie

Bloomington

St. Paul
(state capital)

Rochester

A is for **awesome** Segway tours around Minneapolis when it's sunny.

B is for our state **bird.**

The common loon sings songs cheerful and funny.

C is for the **Como Park Conservatory,**

where big, colorful flowers are always in bloom.

D is for discovery.

At our Science Museum, there is really cool stuff in every room.

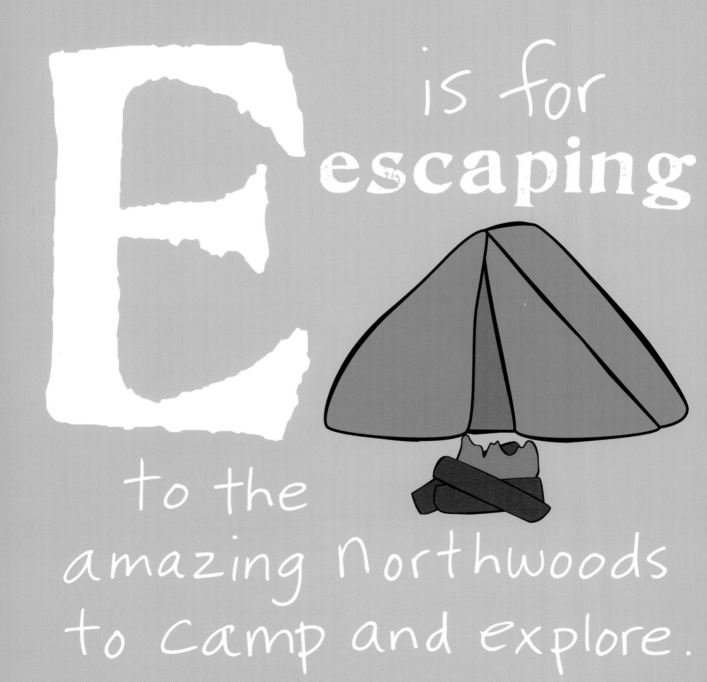

E is for **escaping**
to the amazing Northwoods to camp and explore.

F is for our state **fruit.** You can pick Honeycrisp apples on trees galore!

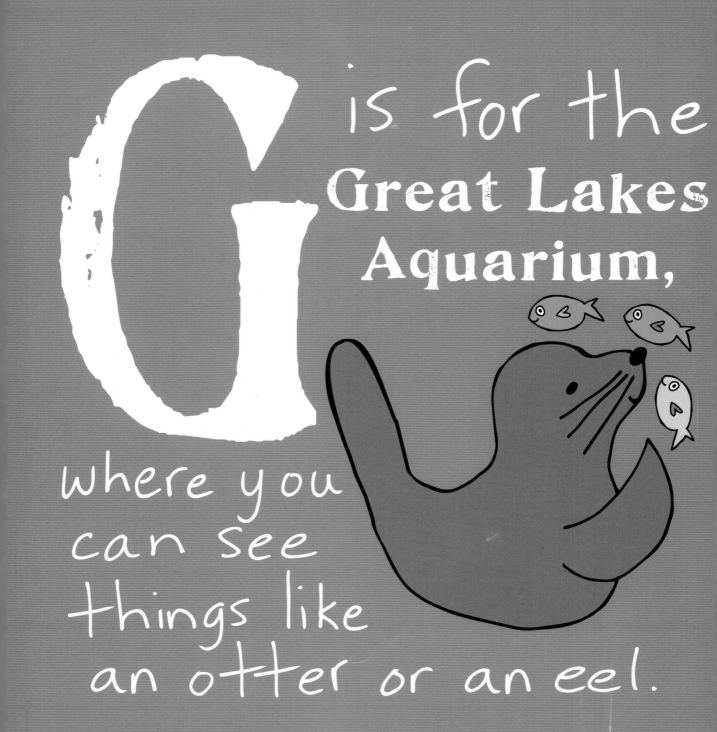

G is for the Great Lakes Aquarium, where you can see things like an otter or an eel.

H is for **hotdish**

served on a chilly day.
With tater tots it's
a comforting meal!

I is for our **incredible** forests. Look for the moose with antlers in many sizes.

J is for the **Jackson Street Roundhouse,** where we learn that choo-choo trains are full of surprises!

K is for kayaking

on Lake Superior on a warm summer day.

L is for our lakes,

like Winnibigoshish and mille Lacs, where we fish and play.

M is for the Mall of America,

where you can shop and ride a roller coaster all in one spot!

N

is for **nice,** because "Minnesota nice" is real, and being kind to others sure means a lot!

O is for our orchestras, where you can hear pretty music on many a night.

P is for the pink and white lady's slipper. Our state flower is a showy sight.

R is for the Minnesota River. It is one of the longest in our state.

S is for our **state fair,** where the food is super and rides are a blast.

T is for Target Field,

Target Field, where the Twins send baseballs flying high and fast.

Twins

U

is for hiking **up** hills at Taylors Falls with family and friends on a nice day.

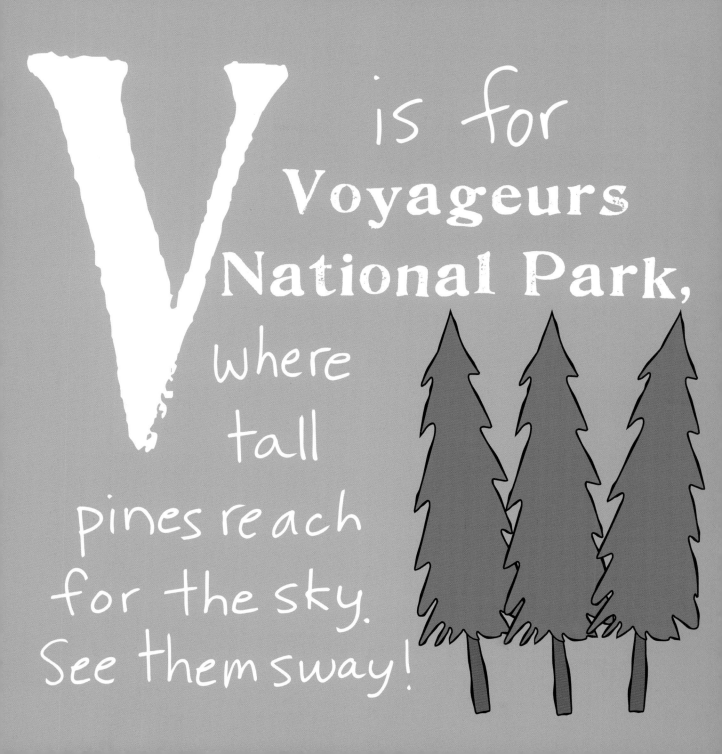

V is for Voyageurs National Park, where tall pines reach for the sky. See them sway!

W

is for
Water Park
of America.
go for a
fun, wet
and wild
ride.

X is for **XOXO**

'cause Minnesotans like to spread lots of love far and wide!

Y is for yummy!

Our state is filled with blueberries, raspberries and blackberries too.

Z is for watching the **zebras** run around and play at the Como Park Zoo.

And now our big
has come to
but you
back to
begin

adventure

an end,
can go
A and
again!

Sandra Magsamen is a best-selling and award-winning artist, author and designer whose meaningful and message-driven art has touched millions of lives, one heart at a time. She loves to travel and has had many awesome adventures around the world. For now, she lives happily and artfully in Vermont with her family and their dog, Olive.

A big thank you to my amazing studio team of Hannah Barry and Karen Botti. Their creativity, research tenacity and spirit of adventure have been invaluable as we crafted the ABC adventure series.

Sandra Magsamen

Text and illustrations © 2016 Hanny Girl Productions, Inc. www.sandramagsamen.com
Exclusively represented by Mixed Media Group, Inc. NY, NY.
Cover and internal design © 2016 by Sandra Magsamen

Sourcebooks and the colophon are registered trademarks of Sourcebooks, Inc.

All rights reserved. No part of this book may be reproduced in any form or by any electronic or mechanical means including information storage and retrieval systems—except in the case of brief quotations embodied in critical articles or reviews—without permission in writing from its publisher, Sourcebooks, Inc.

Published by Sourcebooks Jabberwocky, an imprint of Sourcebooks, Inc.
P.O. Box 4410, Naperville, Illinois 60567-4410
(630) 961-3900
Fax: (630) 961-2168
www.sourcebooks.com

Library of Congress Cataloging-in-Publication data is on file with the publisher.

Source of Production: Leo Paper, Heshan City, Guangdong Province, China.
Date of Production: November 2015
Run Number: 5004881

Printed and bound in China.
LEO 10 9 8 7 6 5 4 3 2 1

The North Star State

International Falls

Bemidji

Duluth

St. Cloud

Science Museum of Minnesota

Twins

Minneapolis

St. Paul
(state capital)

Eden
Prairie

Bloomington

Rochester

1858
ESTOILE DU NORD

MINNESOTA

ABCDE

LMNOP

VWXYZ

FGHIJK